THE-HOUSE-WHERE-NOBODY-LIVES

The kitten ran across the street and came to a stop in the yard of the-house-where-nobody-lives.

"Oh! Don't go there!" Phoebe shouted.

"Don't go there!" Mary called, trotting after Phoebe, who had longer legs.

"Not there!" Tatty was last of all.

The-house-where-nobody-lives sat mysterious and silent in the gloomy light of the cloudy end of summer day.

Once on the steps, the kitten scampered across the porch toward the front door.

"Don't! Don't!" Phoebe sprinted across the yard at top speed.

At the foot of the porch steps she stopped. The front door of the house was opening . . . slowly . . . slowly . . . slowly. All within looked dark and spooky.

"Don't!" Phoebe called again. But the kitten ran in through the opening door. Then the door closed behind it with a quick, rushing sound.

As the horrified girls stood by the porch steps, the door began to open again . . . slowly . . . slowly . . . slowly. No kitten appeared.

Very carefully, one step at a time, the girls climbed up onto the porch. And finally they got across the porch to the open door—and then through the door right into the house.

The door instantly slammed shut behind them with a terrible crash. . . .

Miss Know It All
and the
Magic House

A Butterfield Square Story

by Carol Beach York

Illustrated by Catherine Stock

A BANTAM SKYLARK BOOK®
TORONTO • NEW YORK • LONDON • SYDNEY • AUCKLAND

RL 4, 008–012

MISS KNOW IT ALL AND THE MAGIC HOUSE
A Bantam Skylark Book / January 1989

Skylark Books is a registered trademark of Bantam Books, a division of Bantam Doubleday Dell Publishing Group, Inc. Registered in U.S. Patent and Trademark Office and elsewhere.

ISBN 0-553-15649-7

Published simultaneously in the United States and Canada

Bantam Books are published by Bantam Books, a division of Bantam Doubleday Dell Publishing Group, Inc. Its trademark, consisting of the words "Bantam Books" and the portrayal of a rooster, is Registered in U.S. Patent and Trademark Office and in other countries. Marca Registrada. Bantam Books, 666 Fifth Avenue, New York, New York 10103.

PRINTED IN THE UNITED STATES OF AMERICA

S   0 9 8 7 6 5 4 3 2 1

Contents

1

The-House-Where-Nobody-Lives

Summer was ending. Already a few leaves were starting to flutter down from the trees in Butterfield Square. The leaves were pale yellow, and they lay along the curbs and on the lawns of the fine old brick houses. Some leaves fluttered down and floated on the water of the pretty stone fountain in the park.

Twenty-eight little girls lived in Number 18 Butterfield Square, *The Good Day Orphanage For Girls*, and they often played in the park on summer days. They saw the leaves falling and knew that summer was ending. It had been a wonderful summer. They had eaten Popsicles and planted a flower garden by the front fence. They had had their wonderful Good Day Gold Star Three Ring Circus! But now summer was almost over. Miss Lavender and Miss Plum, the two ladies who took care of the twenty-eight girls, had already mentioned school.

"School will be starting soon," they had said.

Some of the girls were happy that school would be starting. Some were not so happy.

But the girls didn't really have to think about school just yet. There were a few summer days left, fading though they might be. And one afternoon four of *The Good Day* girls, playing at the far side of the park, saw the-house-where-nobody-lives with a For Sale sign on the front lawn that had not been there before.

The girls hurried over to give this sign a closer look. Yes, it said For Sale. There was no mistake.

"Nobody will buy *this* house," Elsie May said, looking at the For Sale sign with disgust.

Elsie May was twelve years old. She was the oldest of all *The Good Day* girls, and she thought she was the smartest. She thought everything she said was true, just because she said it.

And this time, what she said was certainly true. The other girls were sure of that. Nobody would buy *this* house. It was a very strange

2

house and even looked haunted. As they stood staring at the For Sale sign in the yard, one of the windows of the house slid up slowly and then slid down again, like an eye winking at them mysteriously. No hand had raised the window—unless perhaps the hand of a ghost.

Tatty stared at the window between strands of the dark hair that was always falling in her eyes. Mary stood in silent awe, and Phoebe exclaimed, "Oh, ghost! Ghost!" as she hugged herself with thrilling fright.

"It's too bad," Mary said at last, with a small sigh. She was a freckle-faced little girl with curly red hair. Her face was solemn now. "It's a pretty house."

"Pretty?" Elsie May scoffed. "It's full of ghosts and things. If you think it's so pretty, I dare you to go in."

Mary shook her head gravely.

"I dare any of you to go in," Elsie May said.

Nobody looked very interested in going in. Not into a haunted house full of ghosts. After the window had opened and closed by itself, a light went on in the attic window. Even though it was daytime, the girls could see it plainly. Then the light went off as quickly as it had come. From somewhere deep inside the-house-where-nobody-lives, a clock began to strike with a low, heavy sound.

It was rather scary to hear a clock striking in a house where nobody lived.

Nobody had lived in the house for a long time. As far back as even Elsie May could remember, it had been empty. Now suddenly the For Sale sign had appeared on the front lawn.

When the clock in the house stopped striking, nothing else happened. The house grew very still.

"I dare you to go in," Elsie May said again. She looked at the other girls to see if anyone would take up the dare.

"Maybe I will someday," Phoebe said boldly, tossing her head at Elsie May.

Tatty didn't think she would ever go into the house, and she looked at Phoebe admiringly. Phoebe was nine, two years older than Tatty, and she was always doing exciting things. Mary was nine too, and she wrote poems. Tatty didn't have exciting adventures, or poetic talent; her concerns were more simple: trying to keep her hair tidy and her dress buttons buttoned into the right buttonholes. All four girls had been playing tag in the park, but it was Tatty who had the streak of dirt on her face. She had no ribbon in her hair, though there had only that morning been a nice fresh ribbon. "Ah," Miss Lavender had said, tying the ribbon around Tatty's hair. "See how beautiful you are."

"Why don't *you* go in," Phoebe demanded, looking hard at Elsie May. Elsie May only stroked her long yellow braids. She never lost hair ribbons, and there was a blue ribbon at the end of each braid.

"I don't have time now," she said airily, "it's time for supper." Elsie May had found a silver

wristwatch in her stocking last Christmas, and she was very proud of it. Other *Good Day* girls were still getting dolls and coloring books and roller skates. Elsie May was past all that. She was practically grown up!

Now her Christmas watch said fifteen minutes to six, and supper at *The Good Day* began promptly at six o'clock.

So leaving the house behind, the four girls ran across the park, past the fountain and the row of cherry trees that bloomed in the springtime, past the green park benches and the flower beds and the ice cream man.

Behind them, the front door slowly creaked open at the-house-where-nobody-lives.

And slowly creaked closed.

Then all was silent.

2
Supper Time

At *The Good Day* the clocks were ticking toward six.

The kitchen clock was shaped like a teapot. It was on the wall by the stove. Cook could keep an eye on it while she worked, and her meals were always on time. Breakfast at *The Good Day* was at eight o'clock in the morning; lunch was at noon; supper was at six.

For tonight's supper Cook had made potato salad and green pudding (from a secret recipe), and other good things. Two *Good Day* girls were helping. It was their turn. In the dining room they were putting around the knives and forks and spoons and napkins and salt-and-pepper shakers and glasses for milk. Cook, plump and rosy-cheeked, was heaping cookies on the dessert platter—a very popular platter at *The Good Day.*

The parlor clock, ticking toward six, was enclosed in a well-polished mahogany case. The hands of the clock were golden, and a thin rim of gold circled the clock face. The clock had a place of honor upon the parlor mantel.

There was no fire in the fireplace below because it was August. In the colder months Miss Plum and Miss Lavender liked a warm, cheery fire in the fireplace. They liked to sit by the warm, cheery fire and sip tea. Miss Lavender took hers with two sugars. She was round and ruffled, with fluffy white curls of hair held in place by many pins.

Miss Plum was thin and plain and kind and wise. With her many years of experience she always knew what was best to do for *The Good Day* girls.

On this August evening the ladies sat in the parlor by the empty fireplace and the elegant parlor clock, smiling at each other because they had a secret. It was a wonderful secret . . . but it was not yet time to tell about it.

The twenty-eight girls were returning one by one, by twos and threes from wherever they had been playing. They clattered upstairs to wash for supper, laughing and talking. Some had been playing in the big yard that surrounded the red brick house that was Number 18. Tatty, Mary, Phoebe, and Elsie May had been playing in the park—and discovering the For Sale sign at the-house-where-nobody-lives. Tomboy Kate had been down in *The Good Day* cellar building a cave out of cardboard boxes. Agnes, who got good marks in school and was one of the girls who was happy to know that school was starting soon, had been reading a book quietly in her room. She was the only quiet one.

Washing up for supper was a busy affair.

Hands and faces were scrubbed. Fingernails were examined. Hair was combed. Kate and two other girls had a pillow fight, which had nothing to do with cleaning up for supper.

"Stop that!" said Elsie May. She liked to put herself in charge.

Tatty tried to get a comb through her tousled hair. She rubbed her face with a wash cloth to get off the dirty streak. But she had no hair ribbon to keep back her hair. When she was ready for supper, she was still not quite perfect.

Finally all the girls were more or less clean and ready for supper. The parlor clock struck six, and twenty-eight chairs at the dining room table had twenty-eight hungry girls sitting in them, unfolding their napkins. Miss Plum sat at one end of the table. Miss Lavender sat at the other end.

Cook came through the kitchen door with a plate of bread she had baked herself.

"The-house-where-nobody-lives has a For Sale sign in the yard," Phoebe told Miss Plum.

11

Phoebe's place at the table was next to Miss Plum on the right side. On the other side of Miss Plum sat golden-haired Little Ann. She was only five years old, the youngest of all *The Good Day* girls.

"Elsie May says no one will buy it because it's full of ghosts."

Little Ann's blue eyes opened wide. Her little mouth quivered. She didn't like to hear about ghosts.

"It's a haunted house, right here in Butterfield Square," Phoebe said dramatically.

"Nonsense," Miss Plum said calmly. "Phoebe—and you too, Elsie May"—she nodded down the table to the girl with the yellow braids—"you both know better than that. Haunted houses. Ghosts. You know there are no such things."

Little Ann looked at Miss Plum gratefully. Her blue eyes were still opened wide, but she was glad to hear there were no haunted houses or ghosts.

"There are so," Elsie May mumbled to herself.

Miss Lavender took a second helping of potato salad. Ghosts and haunted houses flitted through her thoughts and were gone. She did not worry about such things.

12

"Elsie May dared us to go in," Phoebe went on, her voice rising with excitement. All the girls were listening now. "She dared us, and I told her maybe I *would*—someday."

Miss Plum was not happy to hear this.

"Elsie May," she said reproachfully. "Daring the girls to go onto someone else's property un-invited? Daring them to go into someone else's house? I'm surprised at you."

Miss Plum made it sound awful: going onto someone's property and into someone's house— *uninvited*.

Girls around the table were silent, looking back and forth from Miss Plum to Elsie May.

Little Ann looked at Miss Plum, waiting for what she would say next.

Tatty and Mary peeked at each other. They had been there. They had heard Elsie May say, "I dare you to go in."

Phoebe stuck out her tongue at Elsie May.

Miss Plum frowned at Phoebe, and Phoebe looked down at her plate. But she was not sorry she had stuck out her tongue.

Finally Miss Plum said: "We do not go into other people's houses, even if they are empty. And—" She paused to be sure everyone was listening. Everyone was, even Cook at the kitchen

14

door. "*And*—there are no such things as haunted houses and ghosts. Now we will all please finish our supper."

Upstairs, at bedtime, Tatty looked out of her bedroom window across the park toward the-house-where-nobody-lives. She couldn't quite see the house because of the trees in the park. In the wintertime the trees would be bare. Then she would be able to see the house with the opening-shutting windows, attic lights, striking clock. And who knows what else she would be able to see going on in the house.

Thinking about it made Tatty nervous. If she could see the house, it would seem closer. She didn't like that idea.

Phoebe and Mary shared Tatty's room. It was a nice cozy room, with three small beds, each in a corner. By and by the three little girls were asleep, even Tatty.

In the parlor, Miss Plum and Miss Lavender were reading a letter. This was their secret. It was a letter from Miss Know It All. It had come in the morning mail, and they had already read it several times. Now they were reading it again, for it was a very important letter. Miss Plum already knew each word by heart.

The mantel clock ticked on. Through the open windows the warmth of the August night drifted in.

But summer was ending.

There were leaves floating down from the trees.

And there was a For Sale sign in the yard of the-house-where-nobody-lives.

3

To The Rescue

The next afternoon was cool and cloudy.

"It will rain, mark my words," Miss Lavender said. She sat on the parlor sofa, with her mending basket on her lap. Spools of pretty threads were lined up in a row, pink and green and purple. Her thimbles were silver and gold. Her shiny needles were all stuck into a piece of red felt cut in the shape of an apple—a gift from Little Ann at Christmastime.

"I think you may be right about the rain," Miss Plum agreed. She peered out of the window at the gloomy day. "Yes, rain for sure."

Tatty, Mary, and Phoebe were playing in the

park under these gloomy skies. They didn't mind, for they had found a kitten under a bush.

"There it goes!" Phoebe shouted, as the kitten bounded away just when Phoebe thought she had it. Through the flower bed of petunias, past a lady sitting on a park bench, the kitten ran, with the girls close behind.

The kitten ran across the street at the edge of the park, slipped through the palings of the fence, and came to a stop in the yard of the-house-where-nobody-lives.

"Oh! Don't go there!" Phoebe shouted after the kitten. Her arms were outstretched to catch the kitten, although it was far beyond her reach.

"Don't go there!" Mary called, trotting after Phoebe, who had longer legs.

"Not there!" Tatty was last of all.

Even though the three girls were shouting at it, the kitten made itself at home in the yard and began to go up the steps of the porch.

The-house-where-nobody-lives sat mysterious and silent in the gloomy light of the cloudy end of summer day.

Once on the steps, the kitten scampered across the porch toward the front door.

"Don't! Don't!" Phoebe sprinted across the yard at top speed.

At the foot of the porch steps she stopped. The front door of the house was opening . . . slowly . . . slowly . . . slowly. All within looked dark and spooky.

"Don't! Don't!" Phoebe called again. But the kitten ran in through the opening door. Then the door closed behind it with a quick, rushing sound.

As the girls stood by the porch steps, horrified to see the kitten disappear into the house, the door began to open again . . . slowly . . . slowly . . . slowly. They waited breathlessly to see if the kitten would come running safely out. "Here kitty, kitty, kitty," Mary called hopefully.

No kitten appeared.

"I'll rescue it!" Phoebe said suddenly. "I'll be brave!" She went up a step or two and looked back at Tatty and Mary. "Aren't you coming along?" she asked.

Tatty and Mary had not thought of coming along. They looked at each other uncertainly. Phoebe went up another step and waited for them. "We can't leave that poor kitty in there," she urged. She wanted to be brave, but she didn't want to be brave all by herself.

Miss Plum had said they shouldn't go into other people's houses uninvited, but the opening door was like an invitation. Come in, come in, it seemed to say, creaking on its hinges.

Very carefully, one step at a time, the girls gradually got all the way up onto the porch. And finally, one step at a time, they got across the porch to the open door, and then through the door right into the house.

The door instantly slammed shut behind them with a terrible crash.

And there they were, trapped in the dark house that Elsie May said was full of ghosts. As they huddled together in the darkness, a lighted candle suddenly appeared on a table and they could see that they were in a small hallway. To one side was a dim and shadowy room that was probably the parlor. On the wall above the candle was a large mirror, and in the flickering candlelight the girls could see themselves reflected in the mirror. They didn't look very much like themselves, however. Tatty looked rather fat and squashed-looking. Phoebe looked very tall and thin, like a stick with clothes and hair. Mary looked so tiny you could hardly see her at all.

"It's not *us*!" Phoebe wailed, as they all stared fearfully into the dreadful mirror. "Maybe we're enchanted!"

"I don't want to be enchanted." Tatty stared at

21

her squashed self in the mirror. This was terrible!

But after a moment they realized that they were still their real selves. Only their mirror reflections were distorted.

"It's the mirror that's enchanted, not us," Phoebe said joyfully.

Either way they were certainly in a very, very strange house. They could hear a bird singing and a clock beginning to strike, and in the shadowy parlor they could see a solitary rocking chair—rocking, rocking, rocking.

4

The Escape

"I want to go home," Tatty said in a wobbly voice that didn't sound like her voice at all.

Mary tried the front door, but it would not budge. They truly were trapped in the awful house. Tatty felt cold prickles on her arms. Behind her straggling hair, her dark eyes were shiny with tears.

Phoebe took up the candle with courage. She held it very far out in front of her the way Miss Plum had said candles should be carried.

"As long as we're here, we might as well look for the kitten," she said. "Or an open door, so we can escape. . . ."

Tatty could hardly believe she was really in this house, and she followed Phoebe and Mary from room to room as they went along in the ring of wavering candlelight, calling, "Here kitty, nice kitty," in timid voices. (They did not want to disturb any ghosts.)

When the clock stopped striking and the bird stopped singing, the house was quiet for a few moments. Then the girls heard the sound of wind rustling through treetops. And when the wind faded away, they heard the sound of waves rolling in from the ocean—the way you can sometimes hear the ocean waves in a seashell. Then silence again.

In the kitchen they found an open door, but it was only a door to steps leading down into the cellar of the house.

They did not very much want to go down into the cellar.

"Do you think the kitten went down there?" Phoebe whispered.

"No, I don't think so," Mary said quickly. "Too many steps."

Phoebe nodded with relief. "You're right," she said wisely. "Too many steps."

As they peered down all these steps, another lighted candle appeared below. It was on a small

cupboard in the cellar, and the cupboard door swung open to show dusty shelves and a spider-web.

"Ugh!" Mary said, stepping back right onto Tatty's toes.

The candle in the cellar sputtered out, and a clock began to strike again. *Bong! Bong! Bong!* The girls looked around anxiously. There was no clock to be seen. The kitchen lay in darkness behind its shuttered windows. Their candle was the only light. They didn't know what to do next, and then they saw something moving under the kitchen sink. Tatty was too frightened to breathe, but Mary gave a faint scream, "Ooooo . . ." And there came the kitten, stepping out from under the sink, safe and sound.

"Get it! Get it!" Phoebe flourished her candle, and huge shadows flew around on the ceiling. Tatty was still too frightened to breathe or move, but Mary snatched up the kitten before it could run away again.

Bong! Bong! Bong! The clock was still striking when the flame of Phoebe's candle went out, and the kitchen door swung open.

"Escape! Escape!" Phoebe rushed toward the open door with Tatty close behind, and Mary with the kitten was close behind Tatty. They ran

out into the cool August day, where it was now
beginning to rain.

They ran away from the house as fast as they
could run.

Across the street.

Through the park.

Safely home to Number 18.

The Good Day had never looked so wonderful!

5
Cook's Story

The girls were wet with rain when they arrived, gasping for breath, at their own kitchen door.

Cook had gone out to shop, and the kitchen was deserted except for Agnes. She had become hungry while reading her book (the people in the book were having a picnic), so she had come down to the kitchen. She was sitting at Cook's worktable eating a piece of bread and butter.

Agnes was a slender girl with gentle eyes and pretty brown hair. She fell in love with the kitten at once.

"Is it ours?" she asked with delight. "Here, kitty, you can have some of my bread."

"Kittens want milk," Phoebe said importantly. She found a blue saucer, and Tatty poured in the milk. Then Mary put the kitten down on the floor and they all knelt around it and watched it lap up the milk with its tiny pink tongue.

"It was starved," Phoebe announced. What a good deed they had done, she thought. First rescuing the kitten from the haunted house, and now rescuing it from starvation.

As the kitten drank its milk, the girls planned how they would ask Miss Plum and Miss Lavender if they could keep the kitten.

"It should have a nice name," Mary said. "And maybe a ribbon around its neck."

Yes, they all thought the ladies would be more agreeable if the kitten had a nice name and a ribbon around its neck so it would look cuddly and sweet, not like it might scratch things or be a bother.

The kitten was black with four white paws, so there was no other name for it but Puss in Boots. "We can call it Puss for short," Tatty said.

That left only the matter of the ribbon.

By and by Cook came in with her wet umbrella. She flapped it a few times to shake off the worst of the rain, and then propped it in a corner to dry.

She was surprised to see a kitten in her kitchen.

"What's this?" she asked.

Phoebe and Mary and Tatty were just beginning to tell her about their adventure, when Kate-The-Cave-Girl came up from the cellar. She was dusty from crawling around in her cardboard boxes. And she was thirsty. She thought she could drink about a million glasses of water.

"We went in the-house-where-nobody-lives," Tatty told her proudly. "And we escaped."

Kate stared in amazement. "Did you see the ghosts?" She was all eager to hear about the house. So was Agnes. Cook listened too. Cook knew all about the house, but she had never been inside. Tatty and Mary and Phoebe were the first.

"There were candles?"

"Yes, and in the cellar too."

"A bird singing?"

"And ocean waves."

"Ocean waves?"

"And a big old clock somewhere . . ."

Everybody was talking at once when Elsie May arrived with her silver wristwatch and her nose in the air.

"I went in the house," Phoebe exclaimed at

once, the moment she saw Elsie May. "You dared me—and I did it. I did it!"

"You did?" Elsie May narrowed her eyes and looked at Phoebe suspiciously.

"Me too," Mary said. "I went in, too."

"Me too," Tatty said. (But she didn't ever want to go in again.)

"You did not." Elsie May shook her head. "You're just making that up."

"We went in to rescue the kitten." Mary dangled the kitten so Elsie May could see. "It ran inside, and we went in to save it."

Elsie May looked at the kitten. Its head drooped and its four black legs hung in the air. It began to wriggle to be free, as Mary shook it at Elsie May.

"You could have gotten that kitten anywhere," Elsie May argued. "You're just making it up about the house. You wouldn't really go into a haunted house."

"You shouldn't go into other people's house, haunted or not," Cook reminded the girls. Then she added, "I know all about that house. It's not exactly haunted, at least not in the way you might think."

"It's not?" Phoebe looked at Cook with surprise.

"Not with ghosts," Cook said. She sat at the kitchen table and the girls made a circle around her. They knew all about ghosts. Some of the girls had even *been* ghosts at Halloween time. They had put on white sheets and haunted the stairway and the parlor and the front hall.

"A long time ago there was this man," Cook continued. "I've forgotten his name. I was just a tiny girl myself at the time. He was peculiar, some said. He built that little house across the park, and he told everybody it was going to be different from every other house in the world."

"I think it *is*," Tatty said softly.

"He lived in the house a good many years. Kept to himself. After he died, nobody ever wanted to live in the house again. People said it did peculiar things, gave out strange sounds and such. And it's stood empty now for a long time."

"But how could he do that?" Agnes was puzzled.

"Yes, how could he do that?" Phoebe was all excited. "How could he make it do all the things it does—opening doors and windows—"

"And clocks, and bird singing," Mary added.

"And strange sounds." Phoebe's voice rose. "And candles just suddenly lighting, and a terrible mirror where we all looked enchanted."

35

"Well, that's easy to explain," Cook said. "He put a magic spell on the house."

Of course. A magic spell. The girls had not thought of that.

They were all silent for a moment, and then Kate said, "But *how* did he put on a magic spell?"

"Ah," said Cook, with a shake of her head. "That's something nobody knows."

They were all silent again.

"Will it last forever?" Agnes thought this would be interesting to know.

"I wouldn't be surprised if it did," Cook said.

Phoebe and Mary and Tatty looked at each other with awe. They had been inside a house with a real magic spell upon it. With birds and candles and ocean waves; with an empty chair rocking; with sliding windows, creaking doors, and a clock striking over and over again.

Not many people ever have a chance to be in such a house in all their lives.

6

The Secret Is Told

In the meantime, while the girls were having all these adventures, Miss Plum and Miss Lavender were preparing a surprise for everyone. They had decided to tell their secret. They couldn't bear to wait any longer.

The secret, of course, was the letter they had received from Miss Know It All and read so many times.

Dear Miss Plum and Miss Lavender,
I have decided to cease my world travels and write a book about all the things I have seen and done. When I thought of settling down—or to put

it better—when I thought of where to settle down, of course you came to mind. You and all the girls at The Good Day. *I thought it would be nice to be near you, and I plan to look for a house in the vicinity of Butterfield Square. Wouldn't it be lovely to be neighbors!*

"Lovely indeed!" Miss Lavender always interrupted the letter at this point to express her opinion. Then Miss Plum would go on reading the letter.

I plan to arrive on the 27th. May I stay with you for a few days while I look about the area and see what might be available in the way of a nice little house? Nothing big, you understand. I need only a small house—with perhaps a small yard to plant a flower garden. Yes, definitely a flower garden.

Until the 27th . . . Your devoted friend,
Miss Know It All

When the ladies had first read the letter, Miss Lavender said, "We must tell the girls at once. They'll be so happy."

But the twenty-seventh was still several days

off, and Miss Plum had a better idea. "Let's keep it our own secret for a few days," she suggested. She knew if she told the girls Miss Know It All was coming for a visit and might actually be settling down forever somewhere near *The Good Day*, nothing would be the same. Routine would be disrupted. The girls would be anxious and fidgety. They would always be asking, "Is it the twenty-seventh yet? Is Miss Know It All coming today?"

"Yes, better to wait, I suppose," Miss Lavender agreed. Miss Plum was very wise and always knew what was best to do. But now the secret was too much for even Miss Plum to keep to herself any longer. And on this rainy afternoon the time had come, she said, to tell the girls.

Miss Know It All had first come to Butterfield Square one spring day. The twenty-eight girls had been at school. Miss Lavender and Miss Plum had been enjoying some music in the parlor: Miss Lavender with her violin, Miss Plum at the piano. They had not been expecting any callers, and when they heard a knock at the front door, Miss Lavender went down the hall with her violin and bow. There, at the door, was a small, neat-looking lady with a black patent-leather pocketbook as shiny as new shoes.

"My card," she said, whisking a small white card from this shiny black bag.

MISS KNOW IT ALL
Geography History Arithmetic
Science   Spelling
Recipes, Riddles, and Weather Reports
Reasonable Rates

Miss Know It All really knew all these things. And more. And she had come to *The Good Day* to give a free demonstration of all she knew. When the twenty-eight girls came home from school, she answered questions as fast as the girls could ask: How fast can a bee fly? What makes thunder? Who invented the telephone? What is the population of Iceland? How do you make invisible ink? And Miss Know It All answered riddles too: What has teeth, but can't eat? What has an eye, but can't see? What has four legs and one foot?

Miss Know It All had been to visit at *The Good Day* several times since, and every time she came everyone was happy to see her, and she was always happy to answer questions.

She had a brother Albert, who had once come instantly from Africa when she needed him. She

42

had a box of chocolate candy that was never empty no matter how much was eaten. And she had a beau named William Wise whom she was not quite yet ready to marry . . . although she might someday, perhaps.

Now as Miss Plum and Miss Lavender made the decision to share their secret letter with the girls and Cook, a yellow head appeared around the parlor doorway. Under the yellow hair were two big blue eyes. It was Little Ann. Little Ann was often sent when special favors were requested. She was very small and huggable, and if Little Ann asked for anything, it was hard for Miss Lavender and Miss Plum to say no.

The girls had hunted up Little Ann and given her the kitten to carry into the parlor.

"We have a surprise for you," Little Ann said, holding up Puss in Boots with a pink ribbon around its furry neck. Phoebe had told her exactly what to say. And there, close behind Little Ann, was Phoebe herself—and Tatty and Mary and Agnes and Kate and Elsie May.

Little Ann put the kitten in Miss Lavender's lap, where it began to walk around amid the ruffles. "What a dear kitty," Miss Lavender said with surprise. "Wherever did you find it?"

"In the park," Phoebe said. Which was true.

The girls were not sure what Miss Lavender and Miss Plum would think about their going into the-house-where-nobody-lives, so they skipped that part.

Mary gave Little Ann a nudge to remind her what came next. It was all carefully planned.

"Can we keep the kitty? It won't eat much . . . or . . ."

Little Ann hesitated and Mary whispered, "Be any trouble."

"Or be any trouble," Little Ann said.

Miss Plum could see how all the girls were intently watching Little Ann, to be sure she said her part right. When Little Ann had said her speech, the girls waited for the ladies' answer.

"Oh, I think we might keep it." Miss Lavender looked at Miss Plum. "What do you think, Miss Plum?"

Miss Plum lifted up the kitten in her thin, gentle hands and said, "Yes, I think we might. But perhaps there is an owner. You must ask around the Square tomorrow and see if anyone has lost a kitten."

The girls had not thought of this. They looked so disappointed that Miss Plum hastened to say, "But if no one claims the kitten, we may keep it."

"We named it Puss in Boots," Tatty said

mournfully. It didn't seem fair for anyone to take away the kitten after they had given it a name and put a ribbon around its neck. (And rescued it from a very strange house, where terrible things might have happened to it.)

"Do you like our surprise?" Little Ann stood by Miss Plum's chair.

"Yes, I do," Miss Plum said. She looked around at the girls and her face brightened. "And we have a surprise for you."

She held up the letter, which was now a little the worse for wear, having been read so often by the two ladies.

"Miss Know It All is coming," Miss Plum said. "To stay forever."

7

Miss Know It All

Miss Know It All arrived on the twenty-seventh, a cool August afternoon.

More leaves were drifting from the trees. The water spraying in the stone fountain in the park was cold. It was easy to see fall—and even winter—lurking around the corner.

School was mentioned more and more often. "School is almost upon us," Miss Lavender kept murmuring to herself as she hurried along with the mending. A lot of mending and sewing was required to keep twenty-eight little girls together. Twenty-eight pairs of school shoes were bought. Each girl had her new pencils and paper and pens, crayons and ruler and notebook. *The Good Day* was ready for school.

It was just three o'clock by the mantel clock in the parlor when Miss Know It All arrived. She still had her black patent-leather pocketbook, as shiny as new shoes. She sat in the blue chair by the fireplace, sipping a cup of peppermint tea.

Puss in Boots was asleep on a sofa cushion. The girls had asked all around the Square, but no one was missing a kitten. It was theirs to keep.

Miss Lavender was there, with her ruffles and curls.

Miss Plum was there, sitting straight and calm.

Everything would have been perfect . . . except that there was another person in the parlor.

Mr. Not So Much.

He sat stiff and stern, frowning at everybody. That was his way.

Mr. Not So Much was on the board of directors of *The Good Day Orphanage For Girls*. It was his duty to come once a month to *The Good Day* to see that all was well. He rarely found it so.

Mr. Not So Much, upon his visits, found things amiss. He found too much money being spent. Too much ice cream eaten on summer days. Too much wood put on winter fires. Too much sugar in the tea, and too much tea in the first place. Water was a better drink—and practically free.

"Not so much, not so much," he had to say again and again.

He was a bony man, dressed all in black. Now he sat with his fingers in a steeple, frowning down at the carpet. Miss Know It All had come back, and she was not one of his favorite people. (Mr. Not So Much had no favorite people.) Her visits caused commotion, in his opinion, and there was already enough commotion at *The Good Day.* He was sure it would cost money if she stayed long at *The Good Day.* Mr. Not So Much did not take money matters lightly. Money matters weighed upon him like the weight of the earth.

"So you are looking for a house to buy?" Mr. Not So Much directed his attention to Miss Know It All. He hoped she would soon find a house and end her visit at *The Good Day.*

"I walked around the Square just now," Miss Know It All answered, smiling at Mr. Not So Much over the rim of her teacup. "I saw a nice little house, just across the park. Of course I haven't been inside yet, but I'll make arrangements to do that."

"Yes, yes. Fine idea," Mr. No So Much agreed heartily. He didn't know which house Miss

Know It All was talking about. That was not important. Any house would do, as long as she did not linger on at *The Good Day*, drinking tea, eating meals, costing money. He stroked his long, bony nose with a long, bony finger. "Yes, yes. Fine idea," he said again.

And then he was surrounded by girls running in from play—shouting and laughing and jumping! They had found out Miss Know It All was here at last, they came running by the hundreds. Or so it seemed to Mr. Not So Much. Really there were only twenty-seven girls. There would have been twenty-eight, but Kate had fallen asleep in her cave. She was missing it all.

"Miss Know It All!"

"Miss Know It All!"

"Miss Know It All!"

The girls tumbled about, hugging Miss Know It All, hugging each other, hugging themselves. It was a wonderful moment.

Miss Know It All was pink with excitement.

Miss Plum and Miss Lavender were beaming.

Commotion! Just as Mr. Not So Much had expected. "Not so much noise," he said, but nobody heard him amid the din.

At last, when everyone had settled down, Miss Know It All had a chance to speak.

Well, not at once.

"Where's Kate?" Miss Plum asked, lifting a hand to get attention. She could tell in one glance that one of her girls was missing.

"I know." A tall girl named Nonnie raised her hand, and when Miss Plum nodded, Nonnie raced off down to the cellar to get Kate.

There she was, curled up in a big cardboard box, fast asleep.

"Wake up," Nonnie said, jiggling Kate's shoulder. "You're missing everything!"

They came up the cellar stairs, through the hall and into the parlor like a herd of elephants. Mr. Not So Much closed his eyes in despair. Why was there always so much noise and confusion at *The Good Day*? He did his best, but nothing changed. Chaos reigned. Money vanished. Miss Know It All came for costly visits . . . and how much milk was that cat drinking up every day?

When Kate and Nonnie were in place in the group of girls, everyone turned to Miss Know It All; and Miss Know It All told them that she had seen a nice little house just across the park from *The Good Day*.

"It's just my size," Miss Know It All said. "I don't need a big house. And I know it's for sale. There is a For Sale sign right in the front yard."

A For Sale sign in the front yard.

Phoebe and Mary and Tatty looked at each other with strange expressions. Miss Know It All could only mean *that* house, the-house-where-nobody-lives.

"It looks like such a dear little house," Miss Know It All was saying. "I'm looking forward to seeing inside."

Phoebe and Mary and Tatty thought about the dusty cellar cupboard and the spiderweb, the disappearing candles and the empty chair that rocked. They thought about the terrible mirror in the hall. Would Miss Know It All like birds singing and clocks striking and doors opening and the sound of ocean waves lapping against the shore?

"Of course, I'm going to look at other houses, too, if I find any that seem suitable," Miss Know It All said. "But I would like to be as close to you as possible, and this particular house is right here in Butterfield Square. I could hardly be closer!"

The girls who had heard Cook's story looked at each other doubtfully. They too wanted Miss Know It All to be as close as possible. How wonderful it would be to think of her there just across the park . . . but not in *that* house. Miss Know It

All didn't know what a strange house it was. And if she knew, she wouldn't want to live there.

They ought to speak up and tell her. They ought to say, "Miss Know It All, you don't want that house. It has a magic spell on it." They looked back and forth and tried to think of what to do, what to say. But Mr. Not So Much was talking, and they could not interrupt him, even if they had wanted to.

"Ladies, ladies," Mr. Not So Much was saying. "This all sounds like an excellent plan to me. This sounds like an excellent house. Let us hope that Miss Know It All will soon be settled there."

"Thank you," Miss Know It All said. "I have been traveling around so much, answering questions for everyone, it will be pleasant to settle down in my own little home."

"We're so happy that you thought to be near us," Miss Lavender said, clasping her hands.

Conversation flew around the parlor. But, the three girls who had been in the house didn't know what to do. They sat silently. No one asked them, "What do you think? Should Miss Know It All buy the-house-where-nobody-lives?"

After a while, Little Ann said shyly: "Is the house across the Square the haunted house?"

Miss Plum looked at her sharply. "Little Ann,"

she said, "there are no such things as haunted houses."

Everyone laughed then, except Phoebe and Mary and Tatty. They had been inside the house, and if it wasn't exactly "haunted" in the regular way with ghosts, it *was* under a magic spell and it was certainly a very scary house. They didn't think Miss Know It All would want to live there. But they wished she *would* live there, so nice and close to *The Good Day*.

Then Cook came into the parlor with a fresh pot of tea.

"How nice," Miss Know It All said, smoothing her skirt.

Mr. Not So Much looked at the tray to be sure money was not being wasted. He accepted tea, and stared down into his cup with a brooding eye.

"Miss Know It All is thinking about moving into this area," Miss Plum said to Cook.

"Good news, I'm sure." Cook smiled across the parlor at Miss Know It All.

The girls held their breath, but Cook had no idea which particular house Miss Know It All was thinking about. So she didn't tell the story of the magic spell that was upon the house.

8
Magic Spell, Go Away

The next morning Phoebe gathered together most of the girls who had heard Cook's story about the-house-where-nobody-lives: Tatty, Mary, Agnes, and Kate. Phoebe did not include Elsie May. Elsie May was too bossy. When Phoebe had gathered the girls, they sat in a circle on the grass in the backyard and tried to decide what to do about Miss Know It All and the house across the park.

"If we tell her about the magic spell, she'll look for another house," Phoebe began, "and maybe it will be far away."

"The best thing would be for us to find another house nearby," Agnes said.

They all thought this was a good idea. So they went off first this way and then that, looking for For Sale signs in front yards.

It seemed that For Sale signs were hard to find. Every house already had people living in it. There were curtains at the windows and ladies working in the gardens and sitting on the porches and children playing around.

When at last they did see a For Sale sign, it was in front of a big house. A very big house. A house much, much too big for Miss Know It All. However, it was only two blocks from Butterfield

Square. That part was fine. The girls stood by the front gate of this big house and tried to fit Miss Know It All into it somehow.

"Maybe she could only live downstairs and not bother about all the rest," Kate said, looking up at the towering three stories of the great house.

Just washing the windows of this house would take up all of Miss Know It All's time. Not to mention the dusting and sweeping and the going up and down stairs.

"Maybe she could rent rooms," Agnes said thoughtfully.

But Miss Know It All was not retiring from her travels to run a rooming house. All she wanted was a little house and a bit of yard for flowers.

At last, with lagging steps, the girls went back to Butterfield Square to think up another plan.

They sat on the grass again, but as hard as they thought, no good ideas came. They had a problem that had no answer. They were about to give up, when Phoebe got her idea.

"Why didn't I think of it before," Phoebe exclaimed. "It's just the thing!"

"What? What?" the other girls wanted to know.

"All we have to do is get rid of the magic spell,

and then the house will be just a nice ordinary house."

Yes, yes, that *was* just the thing! The girls chattered with excitement at Phoebe's wonderful plan . . . but gradually they grew silent, as another thought came to them: How would they go about removing a magic spell? They had had no practice at magic spells.

"Maybe my magic ring will help," Kate offered, and dashed off to get her treasure box. It was a cardboard shoe box into which she put interesting and valuable things she found. She had a brass doorknob, a clothespin doll, several large green and blue marbles, a top, a china cat with a chipped ear, and many other items. On the lid of the box Kate had written My Treasure Box. It was her most precious possession, and she brought it down to the backyard proudly.

The other girls had seen most of Kate's treasures before, because she liked to show them to everybody. Now she took out a rather large ring tied on a string. The ring had lost its golden shine. It was too large for Kate's fingers, so she couldn't wear it unless she put it on a string and wore it around her neck.

"My magic ring," she said, holding it up for everyone to see.

"How do you know it's magic?" Tatty gazed at the ring swinging back and forth on the string.

"It says so." Kate passed the ring around so that the girls could read *Magic Ring* written right on the top of the ring.

"How does it work?" Agnes was somewhat doubtful.

"I'm not sure," Kate said. "Let's take it over to the house and see what happens."

They hurried across the park and arranged themselves in a line in front of the-house-where-nobody-lives.

"Maybe it works like a wishing ring," Phoebe suggested. "Make a wish, Kate. Wish that the magic spell would end."

Kate closed her eyes tight, held the ring in her closed-up hand, and said: "Magic ring, I wish the spell on this house would end."

She kept her eyes closed a few moments longer to give extra strength to her wish. All the other girls stared intently at the house. The house was silent—and then from deep within came the heavy sound of the striking clock, and a window flew up and down and then up and down again. A magic spell was not so easily broken as wishing on a ring, even a real magic ring.

It was very disappointing.

"What else have you got in your box?" Mary asked. When Kate opened her treasure box, they poked around and looked for other things that might be helpful, but none appeared.

"Abracadabra always works," Phoebe remembered with a burst of joy.

Yes, yes. Abracadabra always works. The girls waited eagerly while Phoebe placed herself squarely in the middle of the yard. "Stand back, stand back," she ordered everyone.

Then she held out her arms dramatically.

"Abracadabra, abracadabra, the magic spell is broken!"

Sunlight slanted down through the trees. Cars rumbled by in the street.

The girls waited hopefully.

Phoebe took a step back and stared at the house.

Inside the house, the clock was still striking. It didn't stop at twelve o'clock, as a clock should. It went right on bonging away. If you kept count, it would now be forty-three o'clock.

A light went on in a window and then went off.

The magic spell hung over all the house, just as it always had.

"I guess it didn't work," Tatty said sadly, as the girls watched the light go on again in the window.

After all this, Mary took a small spiral notebook out of her pocket—her poem book—and began to write a poem. She thought now that since abracadabra didn't work, maybe a poem would help.

While Mary was writing her magic-spell poem, Agnes had an idea. "I read a book once where a boy got changed into a tree by a wicked witch," she said. Her gentle eyes were serious. It would certainly be an awful thing to get changed into a tree.

"The only way he could become a boy again was if someone took a twig from an enchanted pear tree and tapped his trunk three times."

The girls thought about this. They were not sure what an enchanted pear tree looked like, and there were no stray sticks lying around anywhere—pear or otherwise.

Then Tatty did catch sight of just a small little twig at the edge of the yard. "Here's one," she said, holding it up for the others to see.

"Is that a pear twig?" Agnes looked at the little twig closely.

No one knew if it was a pear twig or not, or

even if it was enchanted, but it was the only twig they had.

"Try it," Kate urged. She was recovered now from her grief at the failure of her magic ring.

Tatty did not seem to be sure exactly what to do, so Agnes said, "Here, I'll do it." She took the twig and went toward the house with the other girls close behind, except for Mary who had sat down on the curb to write her poem.

At the bottom of the porch steps, Agnes reached out her small little twig and tapped the steps three times. "Go away, magic spell," she said. "Go away, magic spell."

The door of the house creaked open just a crack. Inside a bird was singing and the clock was still bonging. It was now about ninety-nine o'clock. Maybe more.

The spell was not broken.

"I guess it has to be a real, enchanted pear twig," Agnes said with a sigh. "Or maybe it only works on trees, not houses."

As the girls wandered back from the porch steps, they met Mary coming to meet them with her poem. It was now finished and ready to be read.

"I have a poem," Mary said. "It's called *Magic Spell, Go Away.*"

"That probably won't work," Phoebe said glumly. "If abracadabra doesn't work, how can a poem work?"

"We can try," Tatty said, pushing at her straggly hair.

There is never harm in trying.

So the girls got quiet and let Mary read her poem. It was the longest poem Mary had ever written. There were three whole verses.

Magic Spell, Go Away

> *Magic spell*
> *go away*
> *do not stay*
> *another day*

> *Magic spell*
> *deep and dark*
> *leave this house*
> *beside the park*

> *Magic spell*
> *disappear*
> *go away*
> *far from here.*

When Mary finished reading her poem, the girls waited to see what would happen.

Nothing changed. The spell was not broken. In the house the bird was still singing. The door was still creaking back and forth. The clock was still striking.

Mary's poem hadn't worked. Nothing had worked. They had not been able to make the house right for Miss Know It All.

It was a sad group of girls who turned away from the house at last and headed back to *The Good Day.*

9
The Red X

That night as they were getting ready for bed in their cozy room, Tatty and Mary and Phoebe had to agree; there was nothing to do but warn Miss Know It All about the house. They would have to tell her about the magic spell that was upon the house she liked so much. They would tell her how they had tried to help by breaking the spell—and how they had failed.

It was the right thing to do, but it was a sad decision.

Kate and Agnes came into the room just at this sad moment of decision. They were already in their pajamas, their teeth brushed, ready for bed. Kate had forgiven her magic ring, and she was wearing it around her neck. Somewhere, some-place, maybe when she was grown up, the magic in the ring would work. She would just be pa-tient.

"We're going to tell about the house," Mary said gravely.

Agnes sat down on Phoebe's bed and sighed as if the end of the world had come. "Who will tell her?" she asked at last. "We can't all start talking at once."

No one volunteered to be the one to tell.

"We'll draw for it," Phoebe said, as time passed and no one was volunteering.

The girls watched as Phoebe tore a piece of her new school notepaper into five strips. On one strip she made a big red X with a crayon.

From the table by the window Tatty brought an old glass jar (once labeled peanut butter) and dumped out the pencils she kept there. Phoebe folded each piece of paper carefully and put them all into the jar. When that was done, she shook the jar until the paper scraps were all mixed up. Then she passed the jar solemnly from girl to girl.

First Mary, then Tatty, then Agnes, then Kate. Phoebe took out the last folded paper, and there was the red X.

"Okay, I'll tell Miss Know It All tomorrow," Phoebe promised, making a terrible face. ". . . unless maybe I think of another idea to break the magic spell."

She hoped perhaps while she was asleep wonderful, magical ideas might come to her. But in the morning she woke up without any new ideas. There was nothing left to do now except tell Miss Know It All the truth.

10

"Everything Else Is Just Perfect."

Miss Know It All was up and out early the next morning, even before the girls came downstairs for their breakfast at eight o'clock.

"I have several houses to see, and I'm eager to get started," she explained to Miss Lavender and Miss Plum. Then she scurried away with her shiny black pocketbook hung over her arm.

There was no chance that morning for Phoebe to warn her about the-house-where-nobody-lives.

Cook had plans for a special supper in honor of Miss Know It All's visit, and Phoebe didn't want to spoil the supper with bad news. "I'll wait until after supper to tell Miss Know It All about the magic spell," she said.

The other girls agreed that was best.

Cook was busy all afternoon preparing the special supper. Girls helped—or got in the way—and the whole kitchen was warm and bustling and full of the wonderful smells of the wonderful meal.

Besides Cook's chicken stew, there were hot biscuits and strawberry pies and sweet pickles in a cut-glass dish. It was to be a feast indeed.

Phoebe watched all the preparations rather unhappily, thinking of what she had to do afterward. Kate had left her cave and gone out to roller-skate with Mary and Tatty. Agnes was one of the girls helping in the kitchen, the one in charge of stirring the biscuit batter. Elsie May, because she was oldest, had the pie dough and the big wooden rolling pin (and a lot of instructions from Cook). Rolling out piecrusts just right was not as easy as it looked, although Elsie May would not admit this.

"I can do it," she said with her nose up.

Outside, the day was very pleasant. Leaves were occasionally fluttering down—one here, one there—to remind everyone that fall was coming and it wouldn't be long before it was Halloween and then Thanksgiving and then snowy winter days.

Dressing for supper, Miss Lavender put on her best dress: a marvelous creation with flounces and gold buttons and a wide lace collar. Miss Plum wore a short string of pearls on her plain blue dress, which was about as fancy as she ever got.

Miss Know It All returned in the late afternoon. The girls were called in to wash up for supper, and by and by they began to gather in the parlor.

The strawberry pies were cooling in the kitchen, the chicken stew was simmering on the stove. The long dining room table was set with plates and silverware and a bowl of marigolds in the center.

Miss Know It All sat on the parlor sofa, and held the kitten in her lap. It had on a blue ribbon today and had been out riding in Little Ann's doll buggy.

"Did you have any luck house-hunting?" Miss Lavender asked, even before all the girls had come down to the parlor.

Miss Know It All's eyes were twinkling. "Yes, I think I did have good luck, extremely good luck," she said. "But let's wait until all the girls

are here, then I'll tell you. In the meantime, I can answer some questions, if anyone has a question."

The girls *always* had questions for Miss Know It All. If school had already started, they would have had spelling and science and history and arithmetic questions. How cold does it get at the North Pole? Who invented the light bulb? If you sold six apples for twelve cents an apple, and five oranges and three bananas for twice as much as six apples, how much money would you have?

But summer hadn't ended yet. There were other matters to find out about.

"What do you lose when you stand up?" Kate started off the questions with a riddle.

"Your lap," Miss Know It All answered, without hesitation. She loved riddles. She knew at least a thousand. Perhaps a million.

"Who invented candy?" Sally wanted to know. She was the plumpest of *The Good Day* girls. (Guess why.)

"Let's have some serious questions," Miss Plum suggested. But it was not the night for serious questions.

The girls surrounded Miss Know It All.

"Did you ever see a dinosaur?"

"Did you ever ride in a covered wagon?"

"Do lions dream?"

"Will eating bread crust make your hair curly?"

Then Tatty waved her hand for her turn and blurted out, "How do you break a magic spell?"

Everyone thought that was a good question. Especially the girls who had been trying to do it with rings and twigs and poems.

Miss Know It All didn't answer right away. She looked at Tatty thoughtfully. She looked around at the other girls. They were all waiting for the answer.

"You may remember," Miss Know It All said, sorry to disappoint them, "I don't do magic."

Ah, yes. Now they did remember. Once before when Miss Know It All was visiting, Mary had asked her if she could do magic. Mary wanted to ask for three magic wishes. Tatty was going to ask Miss Know It All to take them on a magic flying carpet. Little Ann was going to ask Miss Know It All to turn the black fence outside into real sticks of licorice. The other girls had their plans for magic, too. But Miss Know It All said she did not know any magic.

Now the girls felt even more disappointed than they had felt the first time. Oh, if only Miss Know It All could do magic.

"Don't you know about magic spells?" Little

Ann asked softly. She had snuggled up beside Miss Know It All.

Miss Know It All smiled at Little Ann. "I suppose I know a little something about them," she admitted.

Filled with fresh hope, Tatty glanced over at Mary. Phoebe hugged her knees! What great luck this was! Kate sat all perked up and wide-eyed, and Agnes put her chin in her hand and stared at Miss Know It All adoringly.

"Well, how do you break a magic spell?" Elsie May prodded, when Miss Know It All still hesitated.

Miss Know It All began to answer slowly.

"It depends on the spell, of course."

She looked around at the girls again. By now all twenty-eight were present. Miss Plum and Miss Lavender were listening with interest.

"Some magic spells shouldn't be broken."

"Really?" Tatty was puzzled to hear this.

Everyone was puzzled to hear this.

"Some magic spells are very nice," Miss Know It All said, "and by chance I can give you a very good example."

Now was the time to tell about her good luck.

"Just this afternoon, before I came back here, I had my appointment to see that house across the

Square. The house that is just the right size for me and has such a pretty little yard for flowers— although it's too late this year, but next summer I'll plant flowers."

Every girl was listening eagerly. They wanted to hear more about magic spells and less about flower gardens.

"A gentleman from the real estate office met me at the house today and took me through. It is a most unusual house, Tatty."

Tatty already knew that.

"I think there is a magic spell on that house."

Tatty already knew that, too.

"A bird was singing—oh, so sweetly," Miss Know It All continued. "And when we were in the kitchen, I heard cowbells tinkling. Only for a moment, but I felt the whole beautiful mead- owland around me in that moment. It was quite delightful.

"And there is a clock—invisible now, though I may see it someday, who knows. It has a lovely, low sound, and it was striking. Not all of the time, of course. Sometimes it was very quiet in the house. That was nice too."

Miss Lavender nodded to herself. So far, the house sounded very good to her. She liked birds singing and the sound of clocks striking. She thought she would probably like cowbells, too, but she couldn't recall ever having heard any. Miss Lavender had lived in town all of her life and had not ever been near cows.

"To continue," Miss Know It All said cheerfully, "the real estate man said I would have no trouble with the doors and windows, as they

open quite easily and often just by themselves, which will save me effort. He said I may hear a piano playing sometimes. Now, isn't that a marvel? I can hardly wait to hear it. When my brother Albert visits, I know he will particularly like that. Albert is very musical. He once played the flute, but I believe he is out of practice now. And he never did have time for piano lessons, although he always said he would like to take some. Having a piano playing will be a special treat for him. And I'm sure there are many other wonderful things I have yet to discover in the house."

She paused for breath.

The parlor was silent for a moment after all this.

"I didn't know your brother was musical," Miss Plum said faintly. Her mind was rather agog with all this information about the-house-where-nobody-lives. She was not sure what to say, and she seized upon Albert as a safe subject for comment.

"Yes indeed, very musical." Miss Know It All nodded. "And as for the house, I wouldn't change a thing. I like the idea of living in an unusual house."

"It would suit you," Miss Plum agreed. "You are an unusual person."

Everybody began to talk at once, about Miss Know It All living in Butterfield Square—*and* in a house with a magic spell. Miss Lavender beamed above her lace collar. Her eyes were shining as bright as her gold buttons.

"So you see, Tatty," Miss Know It All said, when the girls had finally grown quiet again, "it isn't always a matter of *how* to break a magic spell, but *if* it should be broken at all."

Tatty nodded silently. She thought she understood. At least sort of.

"Did you have a particular magic spell in mind that you need to break?" Miss Know It All asked kindly.

Phoebe gave her head a small, secretive shake to warn Tatty not to say anything more. For now the girls were thinking how lucky they had been not to break the magic spell after all. Mary particularly. Oh, what if her magic-spell poem had worked! Miss Know It All would have lost her unusual house. Mary felt guilty just thinking about her poem.

"Do you have a magic spell to break, Tatty?" Miss Lavender prompted. She was finding the whole conversation quite interesting, and she felt somewhat let down when Tatty shook her head and said, "No, I guess not."

Just then Cook appeared at the parlor door.

"Dinner is served," Cook said in a grand manner. It was her moment of triumph.

Then everybody trooped into the dining room and ate the wonderful dinner.

As they were finishing the strawberry pie— each piece with a fat spoonful of whipped cream on top—Miss Know It All said:

"There is one thing I forgot to mention when I was telling you about the house."

All the girls were quiet, to listen.

"There is a mirror in the front hall that will have to go. It gives very strange reflections, not at all to my liking."

Tatty and Phoebe and Mary remembered the mirror well.

"But everything else is just perfect," Miss Know It All said. "Just perfect."

11

Home Sweet Home

Miss Plum figured things out by and by, for she was very smart. Miss Know It All knew all kinds of things out of books, but Miss Plum knew her *Good Day* girls. She was sure the magic spell Tatty had asked about was the very same spell Miss Know It All had found at her little house.

"Did you girls try to fix the house for Miss Know It All to get rid of the magic spell?" she asked Tatty the next afternoon. School was starting the following day, and Tatty had come to show Miss Plum all her new school supplies arranged in her school bag. Tatty's hair was in her

eyes and her dress was wrinkled, but her school bag was very neat.

Tatty nodded timidly when Miss Plum asked her about the magic spell.

They were alone in the parlor, and Miss Plum drew Tatty close and patted her hand—which was not as clean as it might have been because before Tatty arranged her school bag she had been helping Little Ann dig a hole in the backyard.

"It was kind of you to try to be helpful," Miss Plum said. "But sometimes we can't always know what other people will like. Miss Know It All likes the windows going up and down and the bird singing."

"And there are ocean waves," Tatty confided. "And candles."

"Truly amazing." Miss Plum shook her head in awe.

And so in the beautiful, glorious, golden September, Miss Know It All moved into the little house across the park. So close! And forever!

School started, and every morning at eight-thirty, twenty-eight girls in blue dresses with white collars set off for school. Once again, after the long busy summer, the rooms of *The Good Day* were peaceful and quiet. Miss Plum and

Miss Lavender did mending and letter-writing and a lot of things that didn't get done in summer vacation time when all the girls were bounding about. Sometimes they had little afternoon concerts, Miss Lavender with her violin, Miss Plum at the piano. Puss in Boots was their audience.

Occasionally the ladies were disturbed by Mr. Not So Much, whose visits came regularly; he never missed one. The ladies were used to him, however, for he had been coming as long as they could remember and would go on fretting about expenses for as far ahead as they could see. He couldn't be helped, so to speak.

Otherwise, their days were very happy.

Often the girls would stop by on their way home from school to see Miss Know It All for a few minutes. Nonnie thought now that Miss Know It All lived so close, she might help out with homework. It would be no trouble for her, as she already knew everything in the school books. Nonnie thought they had only to ask Miss Know It All, and the homework would be all done.

But Miss Know It All said no, she could not do their homework for them.

"That is your way to learn," she reminded

Nonnie, who was very disappointed, as you may imagine.

Miss Know It All was very happy with the chiming clock and the singing bird and the sliding windows and the piano playing. She cleaned every inch of the house until it sparkled. Even the cellar and the dusty cupboard where the spiderweb had been.

She took down the mirror that gave strange reflections and hung up instead a beautiful picture of yellow flowers that said "Home Sweet Home" at the bottom. The frame was gold, and sometimes a candle would appear on the hall table, shining on the gold frame of "Home Sweet Home."

"Have you heard the ocean waves yet?" Tatty asked one day when she stopped in after school with Phoebe.

"Or the wind rushing through the trees?" Phoebe asked.

"Not yet," Miss Know It All said. "Just think of all the things I have yet to hear and discover in my dear little house."

It was nice for all *The Good Day* girls to know, as they played in the park or walked around the Square to school, that Miss Know It All was right there, so close by, in her little house . . . where at any moment a clock might strike thirty-two o'clock or forty-one o'clock . . . a piano might play . . . or a bird might begin to sing, though you could not see it, or ever would.

About the Author

CAROL BEACH YORK is a writer with over forty juvenile and young adult books to her credit, including the popular Bantam titles MISS KNOW IT ALL, MISS KNOW IT ALL RETURNS, MISS KNOW IT ALL AND THE WISHING LAMP, and MISS KNOW IT ALL AND THE THREE-RING CIRCUS.

Born and raised in Chicago, she began her career writing short stories and sold her first one to *Seventeen* magazine. Her first teen novel, a romance, SPARROW LAKE, was published in 1962. Since then she has contributed many stories and articles to magazines in both the juvenile and adult markets, in addition to her activity as a novelist. She especially enjoys writing suspense stories.

Ms. York lives in Chicago with her daughter, Diana.